The Alphabet of Peculiar Creatures

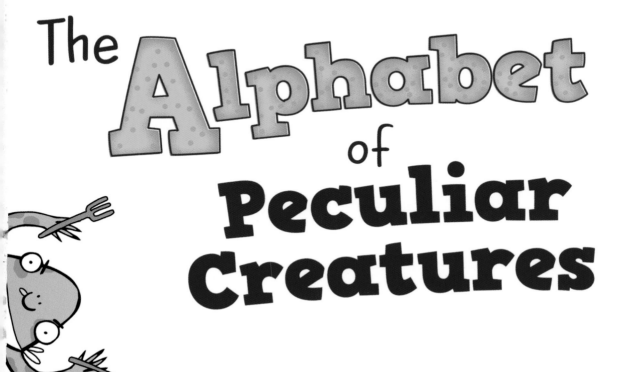

Kane Miller
A DIVISION OF EDC PUBLISHING

First American Edition 2019
Kane Miller, A Division of EDC Publishing

Copyright © Five Mile, 2018
Illustrations copyright © Katie Abey, 2018
Design by Sarah Mawer
First published in Australia by Hardie Grant Egmont

For information contact:
Kane Miller, A Division of EDC Publishing
PO Box 470663
Tulsa, OK 74147-0663
www.kanemiller.com
www.edcpub.com
www.usbornebooksandmore.com

Library of Congress Control Number: 2018942394

Printed in China

1 2 3 4 5 6 7 8 9 10

ISBN: 978-1-61067-834-6

The Alphabet of Peculiar Creatures

of

by Katie Abey

A is for...

AXOLOTL
AXE-OH-LOT-UL

Axolotls are amphibians, related to frogs and toads. They come in many colors, from black to gold, and even pale pink with red eyes!

Axolotls can regrow injured body parts including limbs, their spine, and even parts of their brain.

In the Aztec language, "atl" means "water" and "xolotl" means "dog," after Xolotl, the canine Aztec god. So the word "axolotl" means "water dog."

B is for

BINTURONG

BIN-TOUR-ONG

Binturongs are also known as "bearcats." They are native to South Asia. They give off a strong smell that to humans smells like buttered popcorn.

C is for

CARACAL

KA-RA-KALL

These wild cats are found in Africa and parts of Asia. They can jump into the air and knock down ten birds in midflight.

OH NO!

D is for

DRACO

DRAY-CO

Dracos are lizards that live in the jungles of Southeast Asia. They are also known as "flying dragons."

Dracos have extendable ribs and "wings" that let them glide through the air. When the wings are extended, a Draco can travel up to 30 feet.

OH NO!

Dracos mostly eat ants and termites.

E is for

ERMINE

ER-MIN

Ermines have brown coats in the summer, which turn into white coats in the winter.

F is for FRIGATE BIRD

FRIH-GIT BIRD

Male frigate birds have a red pouch under their necks that they inflate to impress the females.

I'm impressed!

The grimpoteuthis is also known as the "dumbo octopus," as it is thought that they look a bit like elephants!

They live in the deepest parts of the sea and they can change the color of their skin to match their surroundings.

The average size of a grimpoteuthis is 8-12 inches, however, the largest one ever recorded was almost 6 feet tall! That's as tall as an adult human!

H is for

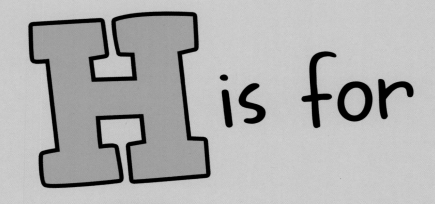

HYRAX

HIGH-RAX

These little mammals might look like big rats, but they actually share ancestors with elephants! Hyrax and elephants have similar teeth, toes and skulls.

I is for

INDRI

IN-DREE

Indri are a type of lemur only found in Madagascar. They make an eerie wailing sound that can be heard up to 1.25 miles away.

J is for

JERBOA

JER-BOW-A

CLEVER!

These creatures live in the deserts of North Africa and Asia. They don't drink water and instead get moisture from plants and insects.

K is for KANCHIL

CAN-CHILL

The kanchil is also called the "lesser mouse deer." They are the smallest hoofed mammal and are about the same size as a hare.

L is for

LOWLAND
STREAKED TENREC

LOW-LAND STREAKED TEN-RECK

These strange, hedgehog-like creatures are found in Madagascar, and have yellow spines that they rub together to make noises to communicate with each other.

M
is for

MARA

MAR-UH

These large rodents are found in Argentina. They might look like rabbits, but are actually a relative of the guinea pig.

N is for

NUMBAT
NUM-BAT

HELP!

Numbats are bushy-tailed creatures found only in Australia. They have long, sticky tongues that they use to dig up and eat termites. Numbats can eat up to 20,000 termites a day!

O is for

OKAPi

OH-KAH-PEE

Okapis are found in Central Africa.
These shy creatures have smelly feet
and can lick their own ears.

P is for

PANGOLIN

PAN-GO-LIN

These armored creatures roll up into a ball to confuse their predators. Pangolins are covered with large, protective scales.

Q is for

QUOKKA

KWAH-KA

Quokkas are small, furry creatures related to kangaroos. They are about the same size as a cat, and always look like they are smiling.

R is for

ROSEATE SPOONBILL

ROW-SE-UT SPOON-BILL

These bright-pink birds develop "spoons" on the end of their beaks as they grow. They use their bills to sift out small bits of food from the water.

S is for

SAiGA

SIGH-GAH

Saiga are antelopes with very unusual noses. They can run at speeds of about 50 miles per hour!

T is for

TARSIER

TAR-SEE-YER

Tarsiers are tiny primates found in Southeast Asia. They can rotate their heads around in the same way as owls. A tarsier's large eyes are heavier than its brain.

U is for

UAKARI
WAH-KA-REE

HEY THERE!

These monkeys live in the Amazon, and can leap over 60 feet from tree to tree! The redder the male uakari's face, the more attractive he is to female monkeys.

V is for

VENEZUELAN POODLE MOTH

VEN-EH-SWAY-LAN POO-DUL-MOTH

This furry little moth is very rare and some people think it's a hoax!

W is for

WOLVERINE

WOOL-VER-EEN

Wolverines look like small bears, and are super-strong and very fierce. They can produce a foul smell in the same way that skunks can.

X is for

XENOPUS

ZEN-O-PUSS

A xenopus is a carnivorous frog that eats its own skin. Tasty! They have slippery skin, and black "claws" on their feet.

Y is for

YETI CRAB

YEH-TEE-CRAB

Yeti crabs have silky fur covering their claws. They live in the Pacific Ocean, and can grow food in their claw hairs!

Z is for

ZEBU

ZEE-BOO

These creatures are a bit like cows, but are only half as tall. They have a large hump on their upper back.